Dragonfly Secret

Dragonfly Secret

•••••••••••

by
Carolyn S. Gold

Atheneum Books for Young Readers

Atheneum Books for Young Readers
An imprint of Simon & Schuster Children's Publishing Division
1230 Avenue of the Americas
New York, New York 10020

Book design by Becky Terhune
The text of this book is set in Aldus roman.

First Edition
Printed in the United States of America
10 9 8 7 6 5 4 3 2 1

Library of Congress Cataloging-in-Publication Data
Gold, Carolyn J.
Dragonfly secret / Carolyn J. Gold.—1st ed
p. cm.
Summary: While trying to stop Aunt Louise from putting Gramps in a retirement home, Nathan and his sister Jessie find an injured fairy.
ISBN 0-689-31938-X
[1. Grandfathers—Fiction. 2. Fairies—Fiction.] I. Title.
PZ7.G5618Dr 1997
[Fic]—dc20
96-10183

For my Mom and Dad

Dragonfly Secret

Chapter one

My grandfather was out in the backyard of my aunt's house, cussing a steady stream of words so nasty it was a miracle the grass didn't wither and die around him, all because the lawn mower wasn't running to suit him. He had to raise his voice to hear himself over its roar, and he raised it enough that everyone in the neighborhood could hear him.

When Gramps can't hear her, Mother calls him a cantankerous old grouch. The corners of her mouth always twitch when she says it, as if she's trying not to smile. She knows he's not really mean. He just likes to sound as if he is.

His name is Nathan, the same as mine, but we always call him Gramps. He once told me he'd lived so long that all his friends were dead. He's eighty years old, so maybe it's true, but most everybody who knows him figures he never had any friends to start with. He isn't what most people call likable, but Jessie and I love him.

I sat on the back porch and fingered the bandage on my arm where I'd scraped it falling out of a tree that morning. One of my eyes was turning black from landing on my head. I looked as mean as Gramps sounded.

Jessie sat beside me on the bottom step, wearing an almost new blue dress with a matching ribbon to tie back her red ponytail. Her ice cream melted slowly beside her. Our cousin Allison sat on the top step, wearing a frilly pink party dress and nibbling the icing off a piece of Gramps's birthday cake.

Jessie studied her spoon. "I wish Gramps wouldn't yell like that."

"He wouldn't use that language if he

thought we could hear him," I told her. It was true. She's eight, and I'm twelve. Grown-ups think there are a lot of things we shouldn't hear. They also seem to think children are deaf.

"*My* mother says it's a nasty habit and only bad people swear. *My* mother says talking like that will make your heart turn black." Allison gave a self-righteous little smirk and returned to digging a cherry out of her ice cream. She was six, but half the time she acted as if she was four. She had every toy Jessie had ever dreamed of, and if she played with them at all, it wasn't when anyone else was around.

Sometimes I wondered if Aunt Louise had bought Allison somewhere, to be sure she'd get a perfect child. Blue eyes, golden hair, never a speck of dirt on her shiny white shoes. Aunt Louise thought Allison was perfect. I thought she was a pain.

"Your mother doesn't know Gramps," I said.

I sighed and jabbed my fork into the big slab of birthday cake on my plate, smearing it around so it would look as if I'd eaten most of it. I don't much like spice cake, anyway, and this one was the main reason we were here, instead of fifty miles away in our own backyard enjoying the lazy warmth of a summer Sunday.

Every year, Aunt Louise insists that we spend Gramps's birthday at her house, even though Gramps lives with us and hates to drive so far. "I hardly ever get to see him," she says in a sweet whiny voice. "He's my father, too, you know."

Every year, Mother gives in and talks him into going to visit his other daughter.

"You know darned well she doesn't give a hoot about me, Kate," he always complains to Mother. "She wants me in a nursing home so she can sell the old farm and spend the money on another highfalutin trip to somewhere nobody speaks English."

"Now, Dad," Mother soothes, straightening the collar on the old plaid shirt he always wears. "You haven't even been out to see the farm in ages. Why should you care? Louise loves you as much as I do. She just thinks that's what would be best for you."

He'll snort and rub his nose, as if the big wart that grows there is suddenly itching something terrible. "If she cared about me half as much as you say, she'd get me something I could use for my birthday for a change. Like a pair of socks, or a new jacket. I never in my life smoked any pipe except the one your mother gave me thirty years ago. Louise should know that by now."

And finally we all pile into the car and make the trek to Hamilton, where Aunt Louise lives in her big modern house with her husband, Edward, the executive, and their perfect daughter, Allison. Just the way we had today.

When we first got there, Aunt Louise fussed about my black eye as if it was something awful. Then we sat uncomfortably around the living room while she told us all about the cute, smart things Allison had done. We all smiled politely, except Gramps, who pretended to be deaf and just sat there frowning. He thought Allison was a pain, too.

After a while Aunt Louise told Allison to get the present she had made for Gramps. She ran off to her room, flouncing white petticoats as she went, and came back with a package that looked as if it had been wrapped for the queen of England. It had gold paper and a gold-and-silver bow as big as a grapefruit. Gramps thanked her more politely than I expected.

"Now be careful and untie that from the back, Father," Aunt Louise said in her whiny voice. "So you can save the bow. I bought it for you specially at Cuthbert's." Cuthbert's is a big store in town that has really expensive stuff nobody really needs. I guessed Aunt Louise thought that would impress us.

Gramps muttered something under his breath and turned the package over so he could untie it from the back. The knots were all under the bow on top, though. After a minute Aunt Louise said, "Here, let me help you," and grabbed it away from him. When she handed it back to him she kept the ribbon and bow.

Gramps tore off the gold paper and Aunt Louise winced. I could tell she thought he should save that, too. Inside was something that looked like a white pancake that had been folded up around a tuna fish can. Gramps stared at it a minute, trying to figure out what to say.

"It's an ashtray, Father," Aunt Louise said, beaming. "Allison made it for you all by herself in her pottery class. Isn't that sweet?"

Gramps looked up, and I think he would have actually thanked Allison, but even she knew what a stupid present it was, and she had gone in the other room to help herself to the ice cream.

"Sweet," Gramps said at last, setting the thing on the coffee table beside him.

Aunt Louise gave Gramps a little package with another big fancy bow on it and said, "Happy Birthday, Father. Edward picked this out for you. I know you're going to love it."

Gramps muttered under his breath while he tried to untie the ribbon. He finally gave up and shredded the paper out from under it, letting the bright blue scraps fall to the floor. Nobody said anything when he eased the present out of the loops of ribbon.

It was a pipe, of course. Aunt Louise always gives him a pipe. He rubbed his thumb along the bowl of it, which was carved like an old man's face, and stared over at my mother, his look saying I told you so louder than any words could.

Finally, he stuck it in the pocket of his vest and stood up. "If I was ever looking to buy a pipe, I'd be sure to see Ed first."

"Edward," Aunt Louise corrected automatically. She took his comment to be a high compliment. I saw Mother bite her lip to keep from saying anything.

"Looked to me as if your yard could use a trim," Gramps said. "Guess I'll take a look-see."

"Don't you want a piece of the cake I baked?" protested Aunt Louise.

"Nope." The screen door slammed behind him, filtering the rest of his words. ". . . poison. Got to keep fit."

Aunt Louise looked from Mother to Jessie to me and back to Mother. "I honestly don't know how you put up with him, Katherine. He's completely impossible. Now he thinks I'm trying to poison him."

Mother laughed. "It's the sugar. He read how it poisons the system. He's all right. He's getting old and set in his ways, but we're used to him."

Aunt Louise didn't look convinced. She started to say something and then changed her mind. "Why don't you children help yourselves to cake and ice cream? You can sit on the back step to eat it while your mother and I talk."

Which is how we came to be sitting on the porch with Allison, listening to Gramps swearing out behind the garage and Aunt Louise raising her voice to Mother in the house behind us, while the ice cream melted into slushy puddles in the bowls between us.

"It's so obvious, Katherine. He should be in a home!" Aunt Louise's words whined out from the front room.

"He is in a home," Mother said mildly. I could imagine her taking a little sip from her coffee cup before she went on. "He's in our home, with his grandchildren. Where he wants to be."

"That's not what I meant and you know it. A *home*. A *retirement home*. Where he can get the best care . . ."

There was a sharp clink as a coffee cup hit a saucer. Mother's voice sounded ominously calm. "Are you saying he isn't getting the care he needs living with us, Louise?"

"No, of course not. But I meant professional care. Listen to him out there. He should be seeing a psychologist. And besides, what sort of influence is he having on your children?"

"Probably the same sort of influence he had on you and me when we were growing up. He's happy where he is, Louise, and we're happy to have him."

I glanced over at Jessie, wishing that Gramps would cuss a little louder and drown out the argument in the house. There are some things kids shouldn't have to hear. It was too late, though. Jessie was hanging on every word, a worried little frown pulling the freckles together on her forehead.

"They won't make Gramps go away, will they?" she whispered.

"*My* mother says he should go live with the other old people where he belongs," Allison chimed in. "She says if your mother won't make him go, she will."

"She can't, can she?" Jessie asked me, her eyes dark and scared.

"Of course not." I tried to sound sure and confident, but inside I wondered. Could Aunt Louise do that? Because if she could, it was as good as done.

Chapter two

"Why are we turning here?" Mother asked as Gramps slowed the station wagon down. We weren't even halfway home.

In the backseat, Jessie sat up and looked around, wondering what was happening. I looked, too, but there wasn't much to see. An unmarked crossroad led off toward some wooded hills and on one corner a small crowd of black-and-white cows swished their tails and stared back at us.

"I figured I ought to go see how the old farm looks while I still can." Gramps sounded sour, and I wondered if he knew what his daughters had been talking about while he mowed Aunt Louise's lawn.

He drove more slowly now that we had left the main highway. There were a few farmhouses along the way, usually set far back from the road so that all we saw were neat brown roofs and maybe the top of a white-painted wall. They were mostly dairy farms, with lazy herds of milk cows grazing in the sunshine. Some of the fields had been planted with hay or alfalfa, and the stubble looked as even and green as lawn.

I remembered when we'd last been out to the farm. Jessie had been a baby, and Dad had walked around with Gramps, saying we ought to all move out there and try to make it a working farm again, with chickens and pigs and milk cows.

Gramps had walked a little quicker, pointing out the spring and the stone silo for storing feed through the winter, and talking about how he and my grandmother had built the place from bare ground and raised my mother and

Aunt Louise there through good times and hard. He had sounded proud, and hopeful. If Dad hadn't been killed in that car accident a few months later we might all have been living there now instead of in town.

"Here we are," Gramps said suddenly, turning in at a broken-down gate between sagging wooden fence posts. The car rumbled across a rusty cattle guard of iron railings set in the ground, and we stopped in front of a small farmhouse with flaking white paint and a blue-gray roof that was turning green with moss. Gramps shut off the ignition and we sat there in the silence for a minute.

"Well," he said after a while, "aren't you going to get out and look around?"

Mother and Gramps went up to look at the house. Jessie and I got out and walked toward the barn, our feet squishing a little in the thin layer of mud that covered the path. There was an old pump in the center of the yard, and I stopped to give the handle a few pulls, up and down, up and down. On the third pull I could hear water, and on the fourth it gushed out, rusty at first, but then clear and clean and cold as ice.

Jessie held out her hands, cupped to catch enough to drink. The water splashed on her shoes, but she caught another handful before she stepped back so I could drink, too.

"It's better than lemonade," I said, wiping my mouth across the sleeve of my shirt.

Jessie giggled. "Maybe it's the fountain of youth and you'll turn into a baby."

"You drank, too," I reminded her. "Mother's going to have her hands full taking care of two babies."

We walked through the barn, breathing the smell of dust and old hay and the scent of animals that had lived here long before we were born. It was dark and cool inside, and a little spooky. The door at the back was nailed shut, but there was a big hole in the bottom, like a dog door. We scrambled through on our hands and knees and found ourselves in an old chicken yard. The wire fence had been pushed down where someone or something had climbed over it, and the gate sagged open.

Across the pasture, we could see a clump of willow trees and a line of dark green marsh plants leading away. "That's where the old spring is," I told Jessie. "Gramps used to catch frogs out there, and fish, too." I wondered if the man who rented the farm now to pasture milk cows ever came down here to fish.

I traced the line of reeds and coarse grass that zigzagged through the center of the meadow and on down toward the fence line, where it ran into the ditch beside the road.

"Let's go see if we can catch a frog."

Jessie followed me out to the spring. The frogs must have spotted us before we spotted them. All we saw were splashes as they dived into the deeper water. The spring was bigger than I remembered, as big as a baseball diamond. There were cattails in clumps along the banks, their furry brown tails beginning to shed sand-colored fluff in the breeze. Here and there I could see big dragonflies, blue and green and as big as my fingers, resting on leaves or hovering over the water like helicopters.

"Let's catch a dragonfly instead of a frog!" Jessie called to me.

I laughed. "Go ahead and try. They're the fastest things you'll ever see when they decide to move."

She didn't believe me, and tried to sneak up on one that was sitting motionless, its four glass-clear wings outspread and glittering in the sunshine. She was inches away when it moved off as sudden and silent as a puff of wind.

I laughed again. "Don't be scared. They don't bite or sting or anything. They'd rather get away than fight."

Jessie came over and sat on the grass beside me. I plucked a blade of grass and showed her how to hold it between her thumbs and blow a loud shriek of sound you could hear for a mile. We both jumped when another whistle answered from right behind us.

"Got you good that time, didn't I?" Gramps said with a grin. "I was going to show you how to make a grass whistle, but I guess I did that before, didn't I?"

I grinned back. "A time or two. This seems like a good place to try it out. No neighbors to bother." I thought of the last time I'd done it at home. Mrs. Pruitt next door had stuck her head out the window and yelled at me for waking up her baby. Gramps had yelled back at her until she slammed the window shut.

"No neighbors at all," Gramps agreed. "At least not the bothersome kind."

Mother came up and put her hand on one of his, like a little girl. "I thought I might find you all out here. I used to love this spot when I was a kid. I always thought it felt like a magical place."

She sighed, and I wondered if she was thinking the same thing I was, that the magic seemed to be working on Gramps. I hadn't seen him so mellow for a long time. I hoped the mood would last after we got back home. It seemed a shame the way he went around angry at the world all the time.

I wished we could stay forever, just sitting there in the sunshine and listening to the drone of the dragonflies and the song of grasshoppers in the lush grass of the meadow.

Gramps tossed his blade of grass aside and looked up at the sky. "Getting late. We've got to be going."

None of us said anything as we walked back to the car. I guess we were all thinking pretty much the same thing, wishing the magic of that moment would never end. We didn't know it then, but the magic hadn't even started.

Chapter three

Gramps's mood grew darker as we left the farm. He was already frowning when he turned out of the yard onto the narrow road, charging off in a shower of gravel. He was scowling by the time we reached the highway. So much for magic, I thought.

"Slow down, Dad," Mother cautioned. "You don't want to get a ticket."

"I was driving before you were born," he retorted. "You don't need to go lecturing me now."

Mother pressed her lips into a hard white line. She didn't say anything after that, even when he turned the corner a few blocks from our house so fast the tires squealed.

As we pulled into the driveway, Mrs. Pruitt's big gray cat slunk across our yard and dived into Mother's flower bed. Gramps yanked the car door open, grabbed a handful of gravel from the edge of the driveway, and threw it at the cat.

"Git out of here, you mangy critter! Go piss on your own porch!"

Mrs. Pruitt was standing on her front step, talking to somebody who looked to me like she was selling lipstick or something. They stared at us, and Mrs. Pruitt looked angry as her dish-mop of a cat came running and jumped into her arms.

Mother's face flushed red. "Go change your clothes and help Dad unload the car, Nathan," she told me as I climbed out.

"I ain't helpless, Kate," Gramps growled. "I can take care of the car by myself."

Mother looked at me and I nodded without a word. It wasn't that Gramps couldn't do it himself. It was just the polite thing for me to help him, even if he didn't act as if he wanted me to.

"He always acts like this on his birthday," Mother said when we were in the house and out of earshot of Gramps. "He doesn't like to be reminded that he's getting old."

I thought of what I'd heard Aunt Louise say that afternoon. I wouldn't want to be reminded of that, either. I'm still a kid, so I have to do what grown-ups tell me to do, but I don't have to like it. I thought it would be twice as bad to be a grown-up and have people make decisions for you, as if you couldn't think straight anymore.

"I'll go help him right away," I said, and hurried to my room to change out of the good clothes I had put on for our visit to Aunt Louise.

We have an old house, with scruffy wood siding that needs paint and a roof that leaks a little over the living room, but it's big enough so we can each have our own room. My room has a window right by the driveway, so I could hear

Gramps bang open the hood to check the oil and radiator the way he always does before he puts the car away.

He started swearing the way he had at Aunt Louise's lawn mower, and it took me a minute to figure out that the car needed oil. It was quiet while he went into the storage shed to get it, and then he started in again, yelling that some so-and-so had stolen the can opener off its hook by the door. I hurried.

Mother shook her head as I went back through the kitchen. "Maybe Louise is right. He's not happy here."

I skidded to a stop. "You know that's not true. He cusses the way some people whistle. It doesn't mean anything."

Mother smiled. "For a twelve-year-old, you're pretty smart."

The angry muttering from the driveway paused, and I heard the sound of running water. "He's going to wash the bugs off the windshield. I can help with that." I ran out the back door, closing the screen behind me.

I could see Gramps standing in front of the car, with the hose in one hand. He wasn't washing the car, though. The water was running down the driveway. He had stopped swearing, and I heard a funny sound. I got almost up to him before I figured out what it was. He was moaning, the way people do when they get real bad news, like they have some horrible disease, or somebody they know died. When I got to where I could see his face, there were tears streaming down his cheeks.

"Gramps! What's the matter?" All I could think of was what Aunt Louise had said to Mother. I didn't think she could make Gramps move away, but maybe she could. Maybe Gramps knew it was going to happen.

He turned toward me, still holding the hose in one hand, not even noticing that he was squirting water all over me. I ducked out of the way behind the car. Mrs. Pruitt and the strange lady were still standing next door. They probably thought he did it on purpose.

"I killed her," Gramps said, moaning again.

"If I hadn't been going so fast she might have gotten away, but she couldn't fly that fast. I killed her."

I glanced next door. Thank goodness they were too far away to make out what he was saying. Mrs. Pruitt would have told half the neighborhood Gramps was a murderer if she had heard that.

"Don't be silly, Gramps," I said, turning off the water. "You didn't kill anybody." I'd never seen him like this before. He never apologized, even when everyone else figured he was in the wrong, which was part of why he had so few friends. Now he was acting like the sorriest person on earth. "What are you talking about?"

He didn't answer. Instead, he held out his hand, and I caught a glimpse of crumpled crystal wings and a dark head. A dragonfly, I thought. All this over a stupid bug.

"It's all right, Gramps," I told him, wondering why he thought it mattered so much. "You couldn't have known. It wasn't your fault."

He dropped the hose and cupped his other hand close over the bent wings. "She's dead," he cried, with such anguish that I suddenly wondered if Aunt Louise was right after all.

Then I got a glimpse of what he was holding in his hand. It wasn't a dragonfly at all. The wings were dragonfly wings, dark-veined and clear as window glass. The head was wrong, though. The huge eyes that bulge out and cover most of a dragonfly's head looked more like intricate coils of tiny braids. The front feet, much bigger than those of any insect I'd ever seen, clutched something close to the body.

And the body—

"It looks human!" I blurted.

Gramps nodded, then shook his head. "Not exactly human, Nathan."

I bent over his hands, peering down at the creature. It was certainly no ordinary bug. The body was almost the size of one of Gramps's bony fingers, but it—she—was definitely shaped like a person.

Gramps started to tremble. "I killed her. If only . . ."

I didn't interrupt him this time. I knew how he felt. It was awful to find something so strange and wonderful only because it was crushed on your car. It made me feel as sad as he sounded.

"What did you find, Gramps?" I had been so involved with the strange thing that I hadn't noticed Jessie coming up behind us. I tried to block her so she wouldn't see it, but she pushed between us and peered into his hands. "A fairy!"

Gramps shook his head and opened his mouth to say something, but I never found out what it was, because right then the tiny creature twitched and tried to sit up.

Chapter four

"Mother! Come see what we found!" Jessie called.

Mother appeared at the back door, wiping her hands on a dish towel. "What's up?"

"We found . . ." Jessie started.

"Better just come see, Kate," Gramps interrupted.

She started toward us but stopped as the lady who had been talking to Mrs. Pruitt walked across the yard toward us. "Oh, no. Not now," Mom muttered.

The lady wore a brown skirt and jacket with a red blouse. It wasn't a suit, exactly, but it looked businesslike, somehow, and she had a clipboard with papers on it in one hand.

"Gol-durned salesmen," Gramps grumbled. "Can't never leave a body a minute's peace."

Mom turned to me. "Nathan, have you been playing with the hose again? Put it away, please."

I stared at her. I opened my mouth to say that Gramps had been using it to wash off the car, but she knew that. She looked worried, and I wondered why. It was just somebody trying to sell her perfume and stuff. Why didn't she just say she wasn't interested the way she usually does?

I closed my mouth and put the hose away while she went out to meet the lady. They talked a minute and then went in the house.

Jessie was still standing beside Gramps, who had his hands cupped nearly closed one over the other. "We'd best take this critter somewhere less public," he said in a low voice. "I'd hate to see her treated like some sideshow freak for everybody to gawk at."

Jessie nodded, her eyes wide. "How about my room? She can live in my dollhouse."

Gramps's face softened with the look that usually meant he was about to ruffle your hair with his fingers, but his hands were busy with their fragile captive. "I don't think so, honey. This is a wild thing. It's not used to houses. And it's hurt. We need to put it somewhere it can't move around too much."

"How about my lizard cage?" I suggested. "It's clean and dry and about the right size."

"Ugh!" Jessie wrinkled her nose. "How would you like to wake up in a lizard cage?"

"It's clean! She won't even know I had lizards in it."

"Sounds like the best we can do for now," Gramps said, putting an end to our argument. "We can make other arrangements later." I thought he was going to say, "If the danged thing lives," but he didn't. He started for the back door.

"Nathan, you go in first, kind of clear the way."

I walked into the kitchen. It was empty. The

way our house is built, the bedrooms open off the hall. You can get to the hall from the front room or from the laundry, which opens off the kitchen. I walked on through to the laundry.

I could hear voices from the front of the house. "... so I can get to know all of you ..." the lady was saying.

I went back out and held the door open for Gramps. "The coast is clear," I said softly. He nodded and led the way, followed by Jessie and me. I made sure the door closed without slamming.

We shut the door of my room behind us and I got the lizard cage down from the top shelf in my closet. I had two chameleons in it last year, the quick, skinny lizards that change from brown to green to hide themselves. They got loose a couple of times, and finally Mother made me give them away.

The cage was about a foot wide and two feet long, made of glass, with a screen top that came off. I set it on my desk. "Lizards need sand and water and a branch to climb," I said. "What do we put in for a fairy?"

"About what you'd put for a dragonfly, I reckon," Gramps said. "Water to drink. Maybe some moss and a branch to climb or hide behind."

"I know!" Jessie ran off down the hall to her room. She was back a minute later with some things from her dollhouse: a bathtub full of water, some tiny dishes that were still huge compared to the fairy, and a miniature bed.

"She'll like this," Jessie said confidently as she arranged the tiny blankets on the bed. "The flowers Mother embroidered on the blankets will remind the fairy of the wildflowers at the farm." I guess it was natural for her to think the fairy came from the spring, where we had seen the dragonflies.

"What will she eat?" Jessie worried.

"No need to saddle the mule before you've got somewheres to go," Gramps told her. He settled the unconscious little creature gently on the bed. "Right now she needs to rest and stretch out that wing."

I squeezed closer for a better look. The fairy had stopped moving, and her eyes were closed.

Her body was a golden brown, covered with fine down that looked like velvet. Her upper body, where a person would wear a shirt or sweater, was shiny like a leather jacket. I couldn't tell if it was clothes she was wearing or her natural skin like a dog's fur or a lizard's scales. She was still clutching something tightly between her arms.

"I wonder what she's hanging on to."

"If she thinks like Jessie, maybe it's something to eat," Gramps scoffed.

"Or a doll," Jessie said softly. "I bet she's scared."

"It doesn't look like a doll, Jessie," I objected. "It looks more like a beetle, only smooth, with no legs that I can see."

"Dolls can look different," Jessie said, pouting. "Teddy bears don't look much like people. How do you know what a fairy teddy bear would look like?"

"I guess you're right," I admitted.

I reached in and gently smoothed the crumpled wing between two fingers, being careful not to break or tear it. The main vein across the top edge was broken. "Will it heal?" I asked.

"Don't know," Gramps allowed. "Never had to doctor a fairy before. Best just let her rest."

We heard the sound of the front door closing. "Now we can tell Mother!" Jessie cried, running out of the room.

I put the cover on the lizard cage and followed her and Gramps into the front room. Jessie was bouncing with excitement, but Mother didn't seem to notice.

"Sit down, all of you. We have to have a talk."

We looked at each other and sat down, Jessie and I on the sofa, Gramps in his old stuffed recliner with the worn spot on the arm. Mother paced back and forth three or four times. Then she pulled a chair out from the table and sat facing us, her eyebrows pinched together into a wrinkly line over her nose.

"This isn't easy for me to say, so please don't interrupt. You know Louise has been worried about whether Dad is all right living here with us. She thinks he'd be better off where there are doctors on call all the time and a nutritionist planning the meals and lots of other people his own age."

Gramps said a word he usually reserves for flat tires and stepping in the mess a neighbor's dog leaves in our yard.

"Now, Dad," Mother said, turning to him. "You know as well as I do that she's got reason to wonder. She only sees you once or twice a year and you seem to go out of your way to irritate her. She probably thinks you're getting senile."

"Well, I ain't." His words were emphatic.

"I know that. And the kids know it, too. The problem is, Louise has her mind made up, and she's sure a professional would agree with her."

"Ain't none of her dad-blamed business."

"Of course it is. She's your daughter, the same as I am. She wants what's best for you."

"What's best for me is for her to leave me alone!" His voice rose in an angry shout.

Mother sighed. "I happen to agree with you,

Dad, but that's not the point. The point is, she's talked to a lawyer about being named as your legal guardian. If she manages that . . ."

"She wants to see if she can get me committed!" Gramps exploded.

Mother blinked back tears, and stared at her hands, which were twisting a handkerchief in her lap as if they wanted to strangle it. "It isn't that simple. She can't have you committed, even if she is your guardian. But she would control all your finances. She could make all sorts of decisions for you. And you pay a share of the cost of the house. If you didn't . . ."

If he didn't, we wouldn't be able to afford a house big enough for all four of us. I jumped up. "We can't let her do this! Gramps belongs here with us!"

Mother looked over at me. "Yes, he does. But we can't afford to hire an expensive attorney to fight Louise. Our best chance is to go along with her until we can prove she's wrong about Gramps being able to handle his own affairs."

Jessie jumped up and stood beside Gramps.

"Nobody would believe her. Gramps doesn't need anybody to take care of him."

Mom smiled, but she shook her head. "It isn't that simple, either, honey. Louise isn't trying to be mean. She really believes she's doing what's right. She asked the lawyer to have a psychologist do an evaluation. We're going to have to go through it together, and somehow convince Miss Ryderson that Louise is wrong."

"Miss Ryderson? Is that the lady who was here?" Jessie asked.

Mother nodded. "She does evaluations in the home, instead of taking the" —she stumbled over the word— "the subject into a clinic. Louise wanted me to take you in for testing, Dad. She knew I wouldn't do it, though. She already arranged this before she said anything about it."

Gramps said another of his words, sounding as if he was spitting on the ground.

"That won't help," Mother said firmly. "In fact, that's one of the things Louise is complaining about. She thinks your swearing is a sign that you're unhappy and that you're rejecting reality."

"If they believed that, they'd lock up most of the baseball players in the big leagues," Gramps snorted.

"That's only one of the things she mentioned. She thinks you're hurting the kids, too."

I could see the shock on Gramps's face. I probably turned as pale as he had. Hurting us! Who could believe that? But then I thought of the bandage on my arm, and my black eye. The psychologist had seen that. What would she think?

"Miss Ryderson is the one we have to convince," Mom said, breaking the silence. "She was assigned to the case last week, and she's been talking to the neighbors. That's why she was here today, to talk to Mrs. Pruitt. Apparently, they don't think I'd tell them if you were doing things like that."

He sat there, staring at the floor, with his mouth so tight on his pipe I was afraid he'd break it.

"Miss Ryderson just stopped over to make

an appointment. She's coming out tomorrow to talk to us. Please, Dad, try to be pleasant to her. We need her on our side."

He stood up and headed toward his room. "I'll be on my best behavior." Then, in a low grumble as if he didn't want us to hear, he added, "Like a durned trained seal."

I looked at Mother and went after him. Jessie trailed along behind. Gramps went into my room instead of his. With his hands in the pockets of his old slacks, he gazed down at the broken-winged wonder in the lizard cage. He turned as we came in.

"This ain't the best of times to tell your mother I've been seeing fairies."

Jessie and I nodded. It would be hard enough for Mother to get through the next few days without having to worry about accidentally saying something like, "I've got to go and check on the fairy who lives in Nathan's room." If she did that, we might all be sent away. A psychologist wouldn't understand, not without seeing the fairy.

"Maybe we should tell Mother and Miss

Ryderson both about what we found," I said. "If we show them, they'll have to believe us."

Gramps held the bowl of his old pipe in his hand and pointed at me with the stem, the way you might shake a finger at someone. "We do that and they'll have the critter in a cage permanent, same's they're trying to do with me. Ain't right, a wild thing like that locked up. No, we got to keep still about this."

I knew he was right. The fewer people who found out about her the better. Otherwise, she could end up in a zoo, or worse, in some laboratory cage like a white rat. If she lived, she deserved to be free, back in the fresh green meadows where she'd started.

"Don't worry, Gramps. It'll be our secret. We'll all have to be careful the next few days." I hoped he could remember that, too, and not do something to upset Miss Ryderson.

Chapter five

I woke up early the next morning and went over to the desk to check on the fairy. She had moved during the night, shifting so that her wings were folded behind her and along her back. The broken one jutted out sideways, as awkward as a square wheel on a bike. I wondered if it hurt. She wasn't moving at all, just lying there like a dead grasshopper. She looked pitiful.

Gramps and Jessie weren't up yet. I went to the kitchen for breakfast in my pajamas like I always do, and Mother made me go back and get dressed before she let me eat. I decided ht then, even before she arrived, that I wasn't going to like Miss Ryderson. Our lives were going to be miserable while she was here.

I thought of running away, but it wouldn't do any good. Maybe, I thought, I'll run away later, if they decide to make Gramps leave. Sort of a reverse kidnapping. I'd stay away until they had to let him come home.

Miss Ryderson arrived at eight thirty. She had on a skirt and sweater this time, without the jacket, and she didn't look so official. I decided she wasn't even as old as Mother. I wondered what gave her the right to decide if old people should be put in nursing homes if they didn't want to go. She had a nice smile, though. I knew I'd better try to be friendly for Gramps's sake, so I smiled back.

"Call me Carol," she said when Mother introduced us. "I don't want to be in the way, but I will have to ask you some questions." Just like a policeman, I thought. As if we were criminals.

After breakfast she sat in the living room

asking Gramps a lot of questions. I could tell he wanted to be rude. He usually got up and left if somebody pestered him that way. But he just sat there and answered her as if there was nothing he'd rather be doing.

Jessie and I went into my room and closed the door. We leaned over the lizard cage to look at the fairy.

"She dropped her doll," Jessie said.

The fairy had moved again, as if she had been tossing and turning in her sleep, and one golden brown arm hung down off the doll bed where Gramps had laid her. The thing she had been holding was on the floor next to her. I picked it up with my thumb and first finger, being as gentle as I could. It was about as big as a large raisin, but pale gold, like sand or dry grass.

"I still say it looks like a beetle grub," I said, holding it on the palm of my hand so Jessie could see it. "Maybe a pupa, like a cocoon, only waxy instead of spun."

"Could it be food?"

"You mean, like a fairy lunch box? How should I know? Dragonflies eat mosquitoes and bugs. I suppose she could be carrying it around until it hatches so she can eat it."

"Could it be a dragonfly baby doll?" Jessie asked.

I shook my head. "No, a dragonfly baby wouldn't look like that. Dragonflies don't make pupas. They live in the water and look like ugly, mean worms with ferocious mouths and lots of legs. They keep shedding their skin as they grow, and one day what climbs out of the old skin is a dragonfly instead of a hell-grammite. That's what they're called: hell-grammites."

"But she's not really a dragonfly. She just looks like one." Jessie took the little lump out of my hand. "I'm going to pretend it's her doll and put it in a little cradle." She got a tiny box from her doll things and put in a scrap of cloth. She put the grub-thing on top and folded the cloth over it like a blanket.

"There. Now she'll know we want to be friends."

Sure, I thought. We mashed her on the front of our car, locked her up in a glass cage, and she's going to think we want to be friends because we wrapped her lunch box or whatever it was in a torn blanket. I didn't say that, though. Maybe Jessie was right.

"I think we should find something for her to eat," Jessie said. She acted as if she was playing house with one of her dolls. I half expected her to go get her little plastic dishes and set up a tea party. She surprised me, though.

"Nathan, what do you think she eats? She's too pretty to eat mosquitoes like a dragonfly. Do you think she eats seeds and plants?"

"Maybe. We can't do anything but guess, Jessie. I can't look her up in the encyclopedia, or call the library to ask them. Nobody even believes in fairies, not really. So there aren't any books about them that aren't pretend."

"How about flowers?" Jessie persisted. "She probably doesn't have a long tongue like a bee, but maybe she can reach into big flowers and get the honey out."

"Nectar. Well, maybe."

"I think I'll put in a bunch of things and see which ones she likes."

"Fine. But don't take up too much space. If she tries to move we don't want her to hit anything with her wings." If she tried to move. I was afraid she was already dead, but I didn't want to poke at her to find out.

Gramps knocked softly at the bedroom door and came in as Jessie left to look for flowers. I stood in front of the lizard cage, afraid that Miss Ryderson would be right behind him, but she wasn't. Gramps seemed to read my mind.

"I think I'm on recess or something. Danged woman has more paperwork for me to fill out than I've seen since I got out of the army."

"I didn't know you were in the army, Gramps," I said.

He stumped across the room. "I'll tell you about it sometime. When you visit me in the rest home." He pointed into the cage. "What's that?"

"Jessie put that lumpy thing in a cradle. She thinks it's a doll."

"Doll," Gramps snorted. "Just as likely a suitcase. Or some dumb decorator thing like one of your mother's glass lamps." He always made fun of the lamps. I thought they were kind of pretty. Mother said they gave our living room a touch of class, whatever that meant.

"Where'd Jessie go?"

"Out looking for something for our fairy to eat. Gramps, if it lives, it won't be able to fly with that broken wing."

"Nope," he agreed.

"I don't think it will heal, either. Insect wings are strong and stiff, but I don't think they mend themselves like bones. They seem more like fingernails. If you break one, all you can do is cut it off."

Gramps stood staring at the fairy, cupping the old pipe my grandmother had given him in one hand. After a minute he said, "Wouldn't help none to cut it off. Wouldn't grow back. The critter couldn't fly with only three, and one of them torn at the tip, too."

"How can we let her go if she can't fly?"

He turned to me and put a hand on my shoulder. "Nathan, I don't think she's even going to live. I killed her when I caught her on the front of the car."

"Maybe," I said, suddenly feeling stubborn. "But we have to act as if she's going to be all right. If she dies, there's nothing we can do, but if she lives . . . Gramps, we've got to find a way to fix that wing."

He looked at me for a minute. Then he took his hand off my shoulder and turned back to the cage. The fairy hadn't moved. "You're right, Nathan. It's like everything else in life. You have to do the best you can and hope everything comes out all right. You can't but lose if you quit playing before the game is over."

There was a sound at the door and we both spun around. It was only Jessie, her hands full of flowers. "I told Miss Ryderson it was a bouquet, to decorate our rooms. I even gave her one of the roses. I think she liked that. She says she's ready for the test you need to take, Gramps."

Jessie moved toward the cage, and Gramps started toward the door. "Guess I better get back before she comes looking for me." He stopped with one hand on the doorknob. "About that wing, Nathan. We better do whatever we're going to do tonight, after Miss Busybody leaves. If we wait much longer it may be too late."

I watched Jessie put three or four flowers in the cage. The fairy didn't move. Maybe we were already too late. But we had to try something. I sat on my bed and tried to think.

I never wanted to be a doctor. I never paid much attention to insects, either, the way my friend Brad does. He has a big collection of butterflies and beetles and things. Probably dragonflies, too, though I never noticed. I wondered for a minute if one of his books would tell how to mend a broken wing. Then I shook my head. Brad didn't heal bugs; he killed them and stuck them on pins and labeled them for his collection.

Brad couldn't help. Nobody could. It had to be us. We had to come up with an idea, but what? I knew Gramps had lots of good ideas, but Miss Ryderson was keeping him busy and worried besides. He wouldn't even have time to think about the fairy. Jessie was an eight-year-old girl, with dolls and dress-up clothes, even if she did like to play ball and ride bikes with me.

Maybe I was just a twelve-year-old boy who liked to read and play outside and watch monster movies, but I was the one who had to figure it out. It wasn't going to be easy. The closest thing to fairy wings I knew anything about was model airplanes.

And then I knew what we could do.

Chapter Six

"You've got the beginning of a good idea there," Gramps said after supper. "Only I don't think model glue will do it. Too messy. What we need is some of that newfangled stuff where one drop is s'posed to hold up seven cows and a steam locomotive."

He was exaggerating, of course, but I knew what he meant. "Mother's got some. She used it to fix a broken vase." I hurried to the kitchen to ask if I could use it.

Mother was still cleaning away the supper dishes. "Honestly, Nathan," she said, wiping soapy dishwater off her hands. "If you can't help at least you could stay out of the way until I'm finished." She dug the tube of glue out of a drawer and handed it to me.

"Thanks, Mother." I gave her a little kiss on the cheek, not because I wanted to but because I knew she'd like it. "I'll do the dishes tomorrow night." Her mouth dropped open in surprise. We took turns washing the dishes, and tomorrow was one of her nights again. I didn't wait for her to say anything. I wanted to get back to my room with the glue.

Gramps reached into the cage and picked up the unconscious fairy. He gently stroked her wings until they opened. Then he smoothed the broken one.

"The glue'll prob'ly hold, but that wing won't be much for strength. We need something to reinforce 'er."

"A matchstick?" I suggested.

"Too thick. Make it too heavy and she'd be lopsided. Matches are soft, too. Might get wet and rot away."

I shuddered at the thought. "How about a

toothpick, then? They're thin, and made out of really hard wood."

"Good thinking. Go get us a couple. Make sure they're the flat kind."

"I went last time. Jessie, why don't you go so Mother won't ask too many questions."

"What should I say it's for?"

"What would a toothpick be for? To clean your teeth. Tell her it's for Gramps."

She went reluctantly, afraid we'd do something while she was gone and she'd miss it. We didn't, though. We waited until she was back.

Gramps took the knife he uses to clean his pipe and shaved one of the toothpicks down so it was even thinner. Then he cut it in half so we had two short pieces.

"Still too long," he decided, inspecting them. He threw one in my wastebasket and cut the other in half. "That's more like it."

He looked from me to Jessie. "My hands ain't as steady as they used to be. Gonna need help from both you kids. I'll hold on to the wing. Nathan, you put a teensy dab of glue on the break to hold it. Then Jessie can put a drop of glue on each splice and Nathan'll lay them one to each side of the vein over the break."

"What's a splice?" Jessie demanded.

"The pieces of toothpick, dummy," I told her. "Just do one at a time. It's going to be tricky putting them on exactly right."

"Wait," she said, and dashed out of the room.

I looked at Gramps. "Girls. Where do you suppose she went?"

He shrugged. "Never mind. Let's get that first drop of glue on the break."

The fairy lay as still as death in his scarred old hands. He held the wing out perfectly straight. "Right there, boy, in the crack."

My hands shook a little, but I managed to get a drop on the broken spot. It was a big drop. I wiped away the extra with the other toothpick, careful not to get it stuck.

"Here!" said Jessie. "You didn't wait," she accused.

"We didn't know if you'd be back tonight or next week," I retorted. "Where did you go?"

"To get these." She held out Mother's tweezers.

"Good going!" I told her, for once thinking that she'd had a really great idea. "I'll hold them while you put glue on one of the toothpick pieces."

She squeezed the watery glue all along the brace, much more smoothly than I could have. I picked it up with the tweezers and gently pushed it into place on the wing. It stuck right away. Gramps turned the fairy over and we repeated the process on the other side.

"Now all we can do is wait," Gramps said, putting the fairy back in the cage and arranging her so that the mended wing wouldn't touch anything until the glue dried. "Let's go watch television so your mother doesn't get suspicious."

We sat on the sofa and watched a dumb quiz show. Then Mother made popcorn and we ate it while we watched some comedy. I didn't catch much of the story, because it was finally beginning to sink into my mind that I had a real live fairy in my room. A real live fairy!

At least I hoped she was alive. After the comedy ended I stretched and said I was going to bed.

"Your favorite show is on next," Mother said, giving me a funny look.

"Oh, yeah. I forgot. I'm going to check on the model I was working on. I want to see if the glue is dry. I'll be back before the show starts." I just *had* to check on the fairy.

"I want to see your model, too," Jessie chimed in.

Gramps pushed himself up out of his chair. "Reckon I'll go to the bathroom. Why don't you get us some more popcorn, Kate?"

Mother picked up the empty bowl. "Sounds like a good idea, but we'd better all hurry or we'll miss the beginning of the show."

Gramps and Jessie followed me to my room. The fairy was alive all right. When I switched on the light she sat up and started making strange chirpy noises, like a cricket only fast.

"It's all right," I told her, staying back from the cage so she wouldn't think I was attacking her. She kept chirping and scrambling around the cage.

"She's a mite scared," Gramps said behind me. "Can't say as I blame her."

Jessie pushed her face up against the cage. "She's not scared of us. She's looking for something. I know!" She reached into the cage before I could stop her.

"Jessie, no!"

"It's all right," Jessie crooned. She unfolded the tiny blanket and pushed the little box closer to the fairy. The fairy grabbed the grub-thing and clutched it to her, sitting back on the bed and rocking gently back and forth. She stopped chirping and started to hum.

"Well, I'll be pickled," Gramps said.

"I told you it was her baby doll," Jessie said triumphantly, letting the top of the cage fall back down.

"You're sure onto something, girl," Gramps agreed, leaning close to the glass to peer at the fairy, who was ignoring us now. "But I'd bet dollars to doughnuts it ain't a doll. It's a baby."

Chapter Seven

Mother had to work the next day. She does accounting and taxes, mostly at home, but sometimes she has to go to the businesses she works for. "Miss Ryderson will be here this afternoon, so keep the house picked up and do whatever she says," she told Jessie and me before she left.

I was glad there were still a few weeks before school started. I wouldn't have been at all happy to leave Gramps alone with the fairy, especially with Miss Ryderson coming. It wasn't because I didn't think he could handle things. Like Jessie, I didn't want to miss anything.

We gathered in my room as soon as Mother left, and sat and watched the fairy. She was moving around now, turning her head to look at her wing and fluttering it softly as if it felt funny. It probably did with those pieces of toothpick glued on, but it was the best we could do.

After a while she settled down. She put the little lump on the doll bed and started exploring the cage. She ran her hands over the box as if square corners felt strange to her. She stroked the blanket and stuck her nose close to the embroidered flowers. Then she shook her head a little.

"She wonders why they don't smell like flowers," Jessie said as if she could read the fairy's mind.

The fairy cupped her hands to drink from the bathtub the same way Jessie and I had at the old pump on the farm. Then she touched each of the real flowers and rubbed her cheek against the petals. She didn't pay much attention to the fancy ones from Mother's garden, even the roses, which I could smell all the way across the room. Instead, she tore one of the tiny buds off a clover blossom and put the small end to her mouth. I couldn't tell if she was chewing or drinking. She did the same thing with several more buds and then sat back down on the bed and picked up the little bundle.

"If that's a baby fairy, Gramps, what will it look like when it's born?" Jessie wanted to know. "Will it have wings, or will it be an ugly worm like baby dragonflies?"

"Hellgrammites, you mean," Gramps said.

"That's an ugly name. I don't like it."

"They're ugly larvae," I told her. "Anyway, that's what they're called."

"Don't matter much, does it?" Gramps cut in, shifting his unlit pipe to one side of his mouth so he could talk around it. "She ain't no dragonfly. No telling what her kid would look like."

"Can she fly now, Gramps? Did it work the way we fixed her wing?" Jessie was full of questions today. I was, too, but I didn't figure it would do much good to ask.

"Don't rightly know," Gramps told her. "Don't guess it would hurt to find out. Got to watch that she doesn't get loose, is all. No telling what would happen to her in town like this. Likely a cat would get her."

I closed the door to my room and made sure the windows were closed. Then Gramps moved to the cage. He hesitated. "Why don't you take the lid off, Jessie? You're the one gave her baby back. She'll most likely trust you."

So it was Jessie who opened the cage. I figured the fairy would come out buzzing, the way a bee will when you open the jar you've caught him in, but she didn't. She sat there a minute, looking up. Then she picked up the baby-thing and stood up.

Her wings blurred as she moved them, fast enough to flutter the petals on the flowers in the cage. Then she stopped, and set the baby-thing back on the bed.

"She's not going to try it," I said, disappointed.

"Yes she is," Gramps said. "She just ain't

sure she can do it with that wing, and she's making sure the little one won't get hurt if she falls."

He was right. She set her wings in motion again and lifted off the bed like a helicopter. She flew to one side, though, and bumped into the glass.

"She can't fly," I said, ready to cry that we hadn't been able to help her after all.

"Sure she can," Gramps said. "She just has to get used to that wing. It must feel pure strange."

The fairy stood up, inspected her wings, and then fluttered the mended one. Then the opposite one. She did that three or four times.

"Trying to get the balance right, I expect," Gramps said.

When she finally flew, I almost didn't notice. One minute she was standing in the middle of the cage. The next minute she was still there. Only her wings were moving, and her tiny feet were an inch or two above the floor.

"She did it!" Jessie cried. "She's flying."

"Why doesn't she fly out of the cage?" I wondered aloud.

Gramps chuckled. "She won't take a chance of being separated from that young 'un of hers. You watch."

Now that she was more certain her wing would hold her, the fairy picked up the little bundle and took to the air. We watched her buzz around the room, checking the ceiling, the windows, the door to my closet. She moved fast, but she was thorough. If there had been a way out, she would have found it.

Finally she gave up and settled back on the top edge of the cage, resting with her wings out straight. Anyone who'd caught a glimpse of her then would have been sure they'd seen a dragonfly.

"What do you suppose her name is?" Jessie asked after a minute.

"Ain't too likely she's got one, Jess. Leastwise, not one we'd recognize. I don't know as she can even talk the way we do."

"Gramps is right, Jessie. She hums and

chirps, but she hasn't said any words. Even if she has a name, we probably couldn't say it."

"We can't keep calling her 'the fairy,'" Jessie insisted. "Let's call her Ariel."

I made a face. "That was the name of the mermaid in that movie you made us watch twenty times. Anyway, it sounds dumb. It reminds me of a TV antenna."

Gramps chuckled. "That's what I always thought. Never told anybody, though."

Jessie frowned at me. "What do you think we should do, smarty pants, name her after Aunt Louise?"

"No," I said quickly. "I don't think anybody should be named after Aunt Louise."

"Well?" Jessie demanded.

"I'm thinking. Don't rush me." I thought of all the girl's names I had ever heard, but they all seemed too ordinary. Fancy names like Guinevere or Lilith didn't seem to fit, either.

"How 'bout Willow?" Gramps suggested. "There were a lot of willows down around the spring."

"Willow," Jessie repeated, trying the word out. "Willow is a perfect name, isn't it, Nathan?"

"Sure," I agreed. It didn't matter to me, and anyway it did kind of fit the fairy, who looked like a piece of rain-wet spiderweb caught on a small brown twig. "Willow it is."

Jessie stood up. "Willow," she said softly, taking a slow step toward the cage.

The fairy turned her head to watch, and clutched the little thing closer to her, but she didn't move.

"Willow," Jessie said again.

The fairy gave a little chirp and moved her wings nervously. Jessie stretched out her arm, fingers spread like the twigs on a branch. "Willow."

For a long moment the fairy didn't move at all. Then she darted away like the dragonfly at the spring. Her wings hummed as she buzzed around Jessie's head. After a couple of circles she landed hesitantly on the open hand, at the very tip of one finger, so that if Jessie closed her hand the fairy wouldn't be caught.

"Willow," whispered Jessie.

The fairy fluttered her wings and then folded them across her back.

Gramps sighed, and I realized I had been holding my breath, too. I let it out slowly. Until now the strange creature had seemed like a thing to me. A live thing, but not a person. More like an odd-shaped bug that we were playing some sort of game with, pretending it was half-human and magical.

I don't know if it was the naming, or the way the fairy decided to accept Jessie, but suddenly she wasn't a thing anymore. She was a real person, even if we couldn't speak her language.

The wonderful moment was shattered by the sound of a car driving up. "Miss Ryderson," I said. "We've got to put Willow back in the cage so Miss Ryderson doesn't see her."

"I hate to lock her up," Jessie said sadly.

"She ought to be able to come and go as she pleases."

"I hate it, too," I said. "But it's for her own good." As soon as I said it I thought how much I sounded like Aunt Louise. I looked over at Gramps.

He grunted and stood up. "Guess I better go talk to the lady. Wouldn't want her to get to thinking that way about me."

Chapter eight

"Louise! What in botheration are you and Allison doing here? Kate's at work."

Gramps's voice was plenty loud enough to carry to my bedroom. I froze, looking at Jessie with the fairy still balanced on her finger. Miss Ryderson was bad enough. We would have to keep Willow in the lizard cage while she was in the house. Allison and Aunt Louise were another matter. Nowhere was safe.

"Quick!" I whispered. "Get her in the cage and I'll put it in the closet."

Jessie turned on me. "In the dark?" she protested in a furious whisper. "Willow will be scared!"

"No, she won't. She's a wild thing, Jessie. She won't be afraid of the dark. Besides, would you rather have her scared for a little while or have Allison grab her and start playing dolls with her?"

Jessie looked unhappy, but she slowly lowered her hand into the cage. She wasn't fast enough. Allison pushed open the bedroom door and came in without knocking.

"My mother says you have to play with me. What are you doing?"

I stepped between Allison and the cage, but like Jessie, I wasn't fast enough.

"Why are you playing dolls in that box? Why are there flowers in there? I want to see, too."

I couldn't tell Allison the truth, but we had a rule that we never lied. I told her the first thing that popped into my head. "It's like a little stage. We're going to make up a story. The doll furniture and flowers will be the setting, you know, the place where the story happens."

"Why don't you go outside instead?"

I thought fast. "Making up a story may take

a few days. We don't want to leave the doll furniture outside."

"What's the story about?" she wanted to know. Allison could drive you crazy with questions. No wonder Gramps pretended to be deaf when she was around.

I couldn't think of anything right off. Jessie came to my rescue. "It's about a fairy who loves flowers." She pulled her hand out of the cage and put the cover on. "Let's go to my room. We can get some paper and write the story down so we can read it to Mother tonight."

"Good idea," I agreed, putting one hand on Allison's shoulder and steering her toward the door.

She twisted back under my arm. "I want to see. You have to show me."

I grabbed for her and missed. She had her face pressed up against the glass of the cage. I looked, too, and held my breath, hoping she wouldn't pay much attention to what she was seeing. Willow was nowhere in sight. And then

I saw her, or at least the tips of her wings sticking up behind the flowers.

"I want a rose," Allison announced.

"Fine," I agreed. "But we don't want to mess up the scenery for our story. We'll get you a fresh one from outside."

"A red one."

"All right. A red one. Come on."

We went down the hall and through the living room like a parade: Jessie, then Allison, and me bringing up the rear. Aunt Louise had parked herself in the middle of the sofa. Gramps was perched on the edge of his chair, leaning forward and looking uncomfortable.

"Nathan has a fairy's house in his room," Allison proclaimed as we went through. "He's going to pick me a red rose."

Aunt Louise opened her mouth as if she had taken a bite of dry cracker and got it caught in her throat. Gramps clamped his teeth tight on his pipe.

"We're going to make up a story about a fairy," I explained. "The doll furniture and flowers are for scenery." I pushed Allison toward the front door.

"Don't get dirty, Allison," Aunt Louise called after us, probably not wanting to waste opening her mouth without saying something.

I heaved a sigh of relief as the door clicked shut behind us. That had been close. I followed Allison to the rosebushes and waited while she picked out the biggest, reddest rose she could find. When I broke it off for her, I stabbed my finger with one of the thorns. It hurt a lot.

"Darn," I said, sticking my finger in my mouth.

"My mother says you and Jessica probably learned a lot of swear words because *he* lives here." She said "promaly" instead of probably, but we knew what she meant, and who she meant, too.

"Everybody says something when they hurt themselves," Jessie argued. "Darn isn't any worse than ouch."

I think Allison was going to disagree, but I took my finger out of my mouth and glared at her. "Maybe we should poke you with a rose thorn and see what you say."

She backed off, pouting. "You're mean, just like him. I don't like you, either."

I almost told her that she wasn't very likable herself, when I saw Miss Ryderson pulling up in front of the house. We were supposed to act like perfect angels until she finished her report on Gramps, so I smiled instead.

"I'm sorry, Allison," I said, and then louder so that I hoped Miss Ryderson could hear me, "Would you like another rose? Maybe a white one?"

Allison considered. By the time Miss Ryderson had gone in the house I'd had to pick a whole bouquet of roses: two red, two white, and one yellow. There was only the one yellow one within reach or Allison would have wanted two of those, too.

"I want to play dolls," Allison declared.

We paraded back through the living room. "So nice to see the children playing together," Aunt Louise purred as we passed. "Most of the time there's no one here with them except my father."

Miss Ryderson nodded at Aunt Louise and winked at me. I wondered what it meant.

In Jessie's room we got out all the dolls. I always hated to play with them because it was so boring. Today I needed to keep an eye on Allison, so I stayed. I could hear the murmur of voices from the living room, but it was hard to tell what they were saying.

It seemed as if the afternoon lasted forever. We made up a story about a fairy who loved flowers. Then Allison insisted that we make up another one, about a talking cat who wanted to be on television. It was a pretty stupid story, but she liked it.

Finally, Aunt Louise called Allison into the front room. "We have to go now, dear."

"I have to get my flowers," Allison told her. "I left them in Jessie's room."

I stood in the living room until I decided she had been gone too long. I didn't want her snooping in my room before she left. I started toward the hall to check on her and saw her coming back with the roses.

Miss Ryderson stood up. "I guess I'll be going, too. There isn't much time left today. I'll come back tomorrow."

They all drove off, and I helped Jessie put away the doll things. Naturally, Allison hadn't offered to help clean up the mess. Then we went into my room to check on Willow.

Gramps stood with his back to the doorway, watching Willow climb out of the cage onto one of Jessie's fingers. "I ain't as young as I used to be," he complained. "I can't take all this rigmarole. I ought to let them lock me up and be done with it."

"Aw, Gramps, you wouldn't like that. Besides, what would Jessie and I do without you?"

Gramps growled under his breath, but I could tell my answer had pleased him. I meant it, too. What would we do without Gramps? It was hard to imagine how our lives would change.

I thought I heard a car drive up, but it was too

early for Mother to be home. I decided it must be one of the neighbors, back from shopping or something. I faced Gramps. "Gramps, I didn't tell Allison about Willow. I didn't lie to her, though. I said we were going to make up a story, and we did. I know you don't hold with lying, but I couldn't very well tell her the truth."

He laughed. "I don't recollect either of you two being so nosy at her age. That 'un's as big a busybody as her mother." He leaned against the doorpost, taking his time and lighting his pipe. After a minute he let out a puff of white smoke and looked over at the lizard cage.

"That Miss Ryderson seems a nice enough sort, 'cept for what she does for a living. 'Tweren't for that, I'd be inclined to tell her what's really happening here."

"I like her, too," said Jessie.

"So do I," I admitted. "I don't think we ought to pretend we're different than we really are. She'll make a fair report. Only one thing. Don't say you saw a fairy."

Gramps puffed on his pipe, his eyes still on the lizard cage. "I hate to think what Louise would have said if you hadn't made up that story. She wouldn't believe in a real fairy, but she'd be sure Miss Ryderson knew I did."

"*My* mother says you're crazy," Allison said from the doorway.

Gramps turned so fast I thought he might fall down. "What in thunder are you doing here?"

"I had to go to the bathroom, so my mother brought me back," she said primly. "And I'm going to tell her what you said."

Chapter nine

I think Gramps would have gladly strangled Allison right then. I know I would have. But by the time we got over the surprise of her being there at all she was gone.

"Will she really tell?" Jessie asked.

I nodded. "Allison is the biggest tattletale in the state. She'll tell. What are we going to do, Gramps?"

He shrugged. "Not much to do, is there? Like we did with the little critter, just wait and see what happens." His words were reassuring, but his face was grim.

That night, none of us talked much at supper.

Mother looked across the table at Gramps and asked, "How did the interview with Miss Ryderson go today?"

He grunted.

"She brought him a test," I offered. "But she didn't have time for him to take it."

"Why not?"

"'Cause your sister Louise and her kid dropped by for a chat right about the time she got here," Gramps said sourly.

He stuffed a piece of roll in his mouth and started chewing vigorously, as if to say he wasn't going to discuss it any further.

Mother paused with her fork in the air, halfway to her mouth with a bite of salad. She looked bewildered. "Why would Louise come by? She never visits. And she knew Miss Ryderson was planning to . . . Oh, I see." Her mouth shut with a snap and the fork dropped to the plate with a clink. She stood up and stalked into the front room, where the phone was located.

"Uh-oh," said Jessie.

"Uh-oh is right," I echoed.

"Hush!" ordered Gramps. "I want to hear this."

We strained our ears, but Mother kept her voice low. It was easy to tell that she was angry, though. Then she paused for a minute, and when she spoke again her voice was louder.

"Louise, that's pure baloney. He was probably reading a story to the kids. And even if it were true, you had no business telling Miss Ryderson. Dad could be seeing flying saucers and still be competent to handle his own affairs. You promised to abide by her decision, so keep out of it and let her do her job." The phone slammed down with a plastic thwack.

Mother came back to the table and sat down without a word. She picked up her fork and jabbed the bite of salad into her mouth. We all looked at our food instead of each other and ate as if it might be our last meal ever.

After a minute Mother sighed and set down her fork. "Louise says Allison heard you say you believe in fairies, Dad. Want to tell me about it?"

He chewed a minute, thoughtfully, then swallowed. "Nope." He speared another bite of meat loaf and stuffed it in his mouth.

"Honestly!" Mother stared at him. "Louise hired someone to find out whether you're too senile to handle your own affairs, and told that person that you believe in fairies, and you don't want to talk about it?"

Gramps shook his head. "Why? Damage is done. No sense gettin' you involved."

"But I *am* involved, Dad. What am I supposed to tell Miss Ryderson?"

Gramps fixed his stare on Mother. "Why should she ask you? Ain't Allison's word good enough to get me shipped off?"

"Dad, you know that's foolishness. But if you start acting this way around Miss Ryderson, no telling what she'll think. I'll just tell her Allison lied."

Gramps shook his head. "No. It ain't right to get someone in trouble by saying what ain't so, even someone as pure disagreeable as Allison."

Mother looked at him blankly. "You mean Allison didn't lie? You do believe in fairies?"

"Did she say I believe in fairies, or did she say I said I believe in fairies?"

"Oh, for heaven's sake, what difference does it make? Do you or don't you?"

"Makes a heap of difference, Kate. She did hear me say that I do. That's no lie of hers."

"Did Allison tell her mother about the fairy story we made up this afternoon?" I asked, hoping to ease Mother into believing what we'd told Allison.

"You made up a story about fairies?" Mother looked confused again.

"It's about a fairy who loved roses," Jessie piped up.

"And Allison made me pick half your roses for her, too," I said, frowning at the memory.

Mother looked across the table at me. "Let me get this straight. You made up a fairy story, and Allison was here and knew that. Then Gramps said he believed in fairies, and she heard him. Was it part of the story?"

"Yes," said Jessie.

At the same time I said, "Sort of," and Gramps said, "No."

Mother folded her napkin and pushed her plate away. "I think it's time someone told me the whole story, and I don't mean the one you made up."

I glanced at Gramps, but he shook his head, ever so slightly. We had agreed not to tell Mother about the fairy until after Miss Ryderson was finished, and nothing had really changed. If anything, it would be harder for her to know about the fairy now than before.

"Jessie and I put some doll furniture and some flowers in the lizard cage in my room. Then Allison came in. I told her we were going to make up a fairy story, sort of like a play. The stuff in the cage was the scenery. Then to get Allison out of my room I picked her some roses. After she left, we were talking about fairies, and Allison came back. She didn't hear everything we said. I guess it sounded like Gramps said he believed in fairies. But he didn't exactly say that."

Mother looked at me. Then she looked at Jessie. Jessie nodded. "It was like Nathan said."

Mother looked at Gramps. He glared at his

plate and scowled. "Believe what you want."

Mother got up and stood behind his chair. She put her hands on his shoulders. "I love you, Dad. We all do. Even Louise, in her own way. I don't think it matters whether or not you said you believe in fairies. I don't even think it matters whether you really do. But I am worried about what Miss Ryderson will think. Promise me you won't be cranky with her."

Gramps softened, and said he'd try.

"And Dad, please don't joke with her about what Allison said. She might not understand."

He looked at me and winked. "Don't say I saw a fairy?"

"Right," Mother agreed, missing the wink. She got dessert, and we talked about other things that had happened that day. I went to bed feeling happy, because I thought everything was going to be okay. I slept fine. The nightmare didn't begin until the next morning.

Chapter ten

"Your room is so stuffy, Nathan. Why don't you open the window?" Mother didn't wait for an answer. She opened the window herself. "Now go have your breakfast. I'll make your bed for you."

I couldn't pass up an offer like that. I scooted for the kitchen. I wasn't worried about Mother seeing Willow. She never went near the cage. Lizards and bugs and frogs made her nervous. That's why I'd had to give away my lizards the second time they got loose.

After breakfast Jessie and I decided to check on Willow. As I opened the door to my room, I heard a crash and saw a flash of gray fur. Smokey, Mrs. Pruitt's cat, bounded up onto the ledge and out the open window. "Shoo, you pesky cat," I hollered after him.

Jessie giggled. "You sound like Gramps." Then her eyes grew wide and her face turned pale. "Nathan! The cage!"

I was across the room in three quick steps. The cage lay smashed on the floor. Crushed roses and wet plastic doll furniture were jumbled amid the broken glass.

"Willow!" Jessie cried, kneeling down and reaching for the wreckage.

"Wait!" I ordered. "You're going to cut yourself. Hand me the wastebasket."

I started picking up the mess cautiously, not wanting to injure Willow further if she was buried somewhere under there. I picked up jagged pieces of glass. Then wet roses. Then doll furniture. I sat back and stared at Jessie.

"Willow's not here."

"Smokey got her!" she said, tears running down both cheeks.

I shook my head slowly. "Maybe. But I don't think so. The cat might have gotten Willow, but where's the grub-thing? I don't think a cat would eat that."

I looked around the room. There was nowhere for a fairy to hide.

"The window," Jessie and I said at the same instant.

"She's outside!" I looked at Jessie. "We've got to find her, before the cat does."

We ran outside. How would we ever find her? She looked like a dragonfly, and I had seen dragonflies in the garden sometimes. It was hard enough trying to catch any old dragonfly. How would we ever find the special one that was really a fairy?

Then I saw Smokey again. The cat was slinking around the corner of the house like a puff of smoke, headed toward Mother's rosebushes.

"The flower bed," I guessed. "Willow is used to roses. Maybe she hid there."

Smokey seemed to think so, too. I scooped up a handful of gravel and hurled it at him, but he didn't give up. He hunkered down and went around to the other side of the flower bed and kept hunting. I could see the tip of his tail swishing back and forth.

"Come on. We've got to hurry."

Jessie started from one end of the flower bed and I started from the other. I scratched myself on rose thorns, but I kept going. I was pretty sure we were on the right track because I couldn't get Smokey to leave, no matter how many times I yelled at him and threw sticks. He knew there was something special in that flower bed. We had to find Willow before he did.

"Nathan!" Jessie's cry sounded excited. I hurried over to see what she had found. "Look," she said softly, pointing at a big yellow rose high up on Mother's favorite climbing rose bush. I could see the tips of dragonfly wings. But were they Willow's?

"Willow," Jessie called softly. "Willow, it's us."

The wings fluttered, and Willow's tiny face

peered between the petals, but she didn't fly down to Jessie's outstretched hand.

"She's probably scared," I said. "I would be if that stupid cat had tried to eat me."

"We can't leave her out here," Jessie said. She wasn't crying anymore, but she looked as if she might start in again any minute.

"I'll get the ladder," I told her. "You stay here and keep an eye on Willow."

I grabbed the big garden shears off the work-bench and lugged the ladder out to the rose-bush. I steadied it against the wall and climbed up until I could reach the rose. Holding the stem carefully, I cut the rose loose and handed it down to Jessie.

"Thank goodness you're safe," Jessie crooned to Willow. I sighed with relief and went to put away the ladder and shears.

When I came back, Willow had climbed up onto her finger, but Jessie was still holding the rose in her other hand. "Nathan, come look."

"What is it?" I asked. She sounded so happy I was sure it couldn't be anything bad, but I couldn't imagine why she wanted me to look.

"Her wing looks okay," I said, giving Willow a quick once-over. "That toothpick seems to be working out fine."

"Look at the rose, dummy," Jessie said, gently thrusting it under my nose.

I bent my head to look. Willow hummed with her wings and chirped at me. There, nestled among the pale yellow petals, was the tiniest baby I had ever seen. He wasn't pink, the way human babies are, but palest gold, only a little browner than the rose petals. Otherwise, he looked exactly like a miniature baby boy. Except, of course, for the pale blue wings that jutted from his shoulders.

Chapter eleven

"He was born in the flower bed. Let's call him Sweet William," Jessie said happily.

I sniffed. "No. Sweet William is one of the flowers that makes me sneeze. Besides, no boy would want to go through life being called sweet."

She peered down at the tiny infant still nestled in the heart of the rose. "If you say so. What do you think we should call him?"

"How about Ash? That's a tree, sort of like an aspen or a birch tree. I saw some of them up on the farm."

Jessie shook her head. "Reminds me of what's left after you burn the trash."

I could see her point. The new fairy was delicate and beautiful, like a soap bubble in the sunshine. Ash didn't fit. "How about Reed, then? People usually spell it R-e-i-d, but he's not a person. And a reed is a water plant like a cattail. I think that's where he belongs."

Jessie nodded. "I like it. Let's go tell Gramps."

"Not so fast. What if we run into Mother? We still don't want her to find out about them. And now that the lizard cage is gone, where are we going to keep them?"

We talked about it awhile, and didn't come up with much. Finally I left Jessie with the two fairies and went into the house, going through the back door to the kitchen. I found a big empty coffee can in the cupboard where Mother keeps them to store things in. It wasn't as nice as the lizard cage, but it was big enough and safe enough until we could come up with something better. I took it back outside.

"Let's pick some roses and put them in the can. And some clover blossoms for Willow to eat," Jessie said. She held the two fairies and watched me as I did it. When I was finished she lowered the yellow rose into the can. Willow buzzed in after it and settled next to her son.

"You know, Jessie, clover blossoms may not be enough."

"What do you mean?" she asked.

"We know Willow eats clover. Or drinks it or something. But maybe that's like us trying to live on lemonade. Besides," I added, shifting the coffee can so Jessie could see better, "baby fairies may need something special to eat."

Jessie looked so stricken that I hurried to reassure her. "Willow has done all right so far, and she seems to be happy, so maybe it will be okay. Even so, I think we better figure out a way to get them back to the farm where they belong as soon as we can."

She nodded, looking sad. "I know we can't keep them. Willow's not like a pet. She's more like a friend, even if she can't talk."

We went in the back door. "I'm going to take Willow into my room for a while," Jessie said.

"Good idea," I agreed. "We don't want Mother getting curious about why you spend so much time in my room."

Mother was sitting in the living room sewing

a button on one of my shirts. I nodded to Jessie to go ahead through the laundry room and went into the front room just as a knock sounded at the front door.

"I'll get it," I told Mother. I opened the door. "Good morning, Miss Ryderson," I said politely, the way Mother taught us to greet special visitors. "Won't you come in?"

"Nathan!" I heard Gramps screech my name from the hallway and turned away from the door. "The fairy's gone!" he cried. Then he caught sight of Miss Ryderson and stopped, his mouth opening and closing as if the words were stuck in his throat.

Mother sat stock-still with the mending clasped to her the way Willow had held the baby the first day. It was a wonder she didn't stick herself with the needle.

Miss Ryderson recovered first. "I seem to be interrupting something. Would it be better if I came back?"

"No, no," I said, finding my voice. "Come on in." I turned to Gramps. "It's all right. Jessie took the fairy in her room to work on the story."

Gramps swallowed.

"Honest," I said.

Mother threw her mending back in the basket. "I wish you'd finish that story and do something else," she snapped. "What's wrong with playing ball in the backyard? Every time I turn around you're talking about fairies." Then she seemed to remember why Miss Ryderson was there. "I'm sorry. I guess I got up on the wrong side of the bed. I'm so worried about your report I can't seem to sleep. I'll be glad when that's over, too. Let me get you a cup of coffee."

Miss Ryderson set her briefcase on the coffee table and sat down on the sofa. She looked at me. "Does your fairy have a name?" she asked with a smile.

"Yes," I said with reluctance. "We call her Willow."

"A pretty name. Does she have a magic wand?"

I shook my head.

"How about your three wishes? What are you going to wish for?"

"She isn't magic," I said, wondering how I could get out of this conversation. "She's like a tiny person with wings."

Miss Ryderson laughed. "If I were inventing a character for a fairy story, I'd have made her more magical. What if she *could* grant wishes, Nathan? What would you wish for?"

I looked at her, wondering if she was trying to trick me. I couldn't tell. "I'd wish that Gramps could stay with us," I said at last. "But that isn't up to fairy magic. That's up to you."

She looked down at her hands, a little embarrassed, I thought. "Nathan, I don't decide what will happen. I only make recommendations. Sometimes older people get confused enough to do foolish, dangerous things. It's my job to determine whether they are likely to do things to hurt themselves or the people around them."

Mother came back with the coffee, and I took the chance to escape. I went outside, and sat on the grass beside the flower bed, thinking about the way everyone is always making decisions for other people. Parents decide what's best for kids. Grown-ups decide for old people like Gramps. Even Jessie and I were deciding what was best for Willow and Reed. No matter how sure we were, no matter how much we cared about them, we could never really know what other people thought or needed.

Mother came outside with a pair of scissors. She walked over to the flower bed and looked at the roses. She cut a pink one and two red ones and a couple of white ones. Then she came over and sat on the grass beside me, her knees drawn up under her chin with her arms resting on them.

"Nathan, I think Jessie's been crying. Is everything all right? Is there something you should tell me?"

I wanted to tell her about Willow and Reed. I hadn't lied to her, but I hadn't told the truth, either. I didn't like the way that made me feel. I couldn't tell her, though.

"Everything's fine," I said. "We're just worried about Gramps."

She sighed. "I am, too. Especially this talk about fairies. I think Louise may be right. He may be getting senile."

"Does senile mean you have a good imagination?" I asked.

She shook her head. "No, it means you can't tell the difference between what's real and what's imaginary."

"Gramps can tell the difference. He jokes around and won't say what you want him to sometimes, but he knows what's real and what isn't."

"I hope you're right."

She stopped as Miss Ryderson's voice drifted to us from the open window. "Nathan says his fairy doesn't grant wishes. Do you believe in magic, Mr. Bentson?"

Gramps's reply was muffled, and I guess Miss Ryderson couldn't hear it, either. "What?" she asked.

"I said I don't know," Gramps said, clearing his throat and sounding irritated. "If you mean the three wishes variety, I reckon Nathan's right, ain't likely anything to it. But there's other magic, young lady, and them who disbelieve it and shut their eyes to anything what's not ordinary lead mighty dreary lives."

"Your daughter, Louise, for example?"

"For example," agreed Gramps.

"Do you think she understands you?" asked Miss Ryderson.

"How could she, when we don't see each other any more than a beggar sees lamb chops?"

"Why do you think she asked me to do this evaluation?"

There was a long pause. Then Gramps said, "I reckon you'd have to ask her that."

"I have," said Miss Ryderson. "She seems to care about you a lot, Mr. Bentson. Can you believe that?"

"Louise cares a lot about Louise." He paused again. "Maybe she does care about me, right enough, in her own way. But that don't give her the right to meddle. That's mighty hard to forgive."

"Did you ever think she might be right? That it might be best for you to live with people your own age, with the same sort of interests?"

"Like what?" Gramps demanded. "Like whether my rheumatiz is actin' up when a storm's comin', and whether I'll live to see my grandkids through college? Like how to keep my teeth in so's I can eat an apple, or how to pick up a newspaper off the porch when I can't bend over? I don't rightly think I'd like living in a place where everybody shared that sort of interests, missy."

Beside me, Mother shook her head and stood up. "Eavesdropping isn't right. People hear what they shouldn't." She picked up the roses and went around to the back of the house. I heard the back door open and close.

Inside the front room, Miss Ryderson said something about the recreational opportunities at a senior citizens facility.

"Ain't much to live for, is it?" Gramps asked. "Pinochle and TV shows. Might as well sit on the porch and smoke my pipe until it's time to die."

Mother was right. Eavesdropping wasn't a good idea. I wished I hadn't heard the sadness in Gramps's voice. I wished that Miss Ryderson had never come. I wished more than anything that Gramps could stay with us. If Willow had been a magic fairy, those would have been my three wishes, for sure. But she wasn't. She was nothing but a freak, a cross between a human being and a dragonfly. There wasn't any magic in that to help any of us.

Chapter twelve

"What do you think Miss Ryderson will say in her report?" I asked Mother when the two of us were sitting at the breakfast table alone.

She sighed and turned her coffee cup in little half circles, pushing the handle between her thumbs. "I'm afraid it won't be good, Nathan."

"What will she say?" I persisted.

"Well, let's see. She saw him yell at Mrs. Pruitt yesterday, and throw rocks at her cat. She'll probably call that antisocial behavior."

"But that cat is always in our yard," I objected. "It scratches up your flower bed and does things under the bush by the front window. And yesterday it got in the house and knocked my lizard cage off my desk and broke it."

"Doesn't matter," Mother said, her face glum. "It shows he doesn't get along with other people."

"He gets along fine with us."

"That's different, Nathan. We're his family."

"If he doesn't get along with people, why should he go live where there are lots of people around instead of only a few?" I demanded. "It doesn't make sense."

Mother looked at me. "No, it doesn't, does it?" She sounded sad.

"What else will Miss Ryderson say?"

"That he thinks Louise is trying to get him committed."

"She is."

"Well, yes, but not because she wants to hurt him."

I frowned. "She doesn't care about him at all. All she wants is the money from the farm. That hurts him a lot."

Mother's eyes were wide and serious. "So you believe that, too."

I swallowed a mouthful of cereal. "She's always saying he ought to sell the old farm. Why else would she say that?"

"Because she thought it was costing your grandfather too much money. Until a few weeks ago she didn't even know it was rented for pasture. She thought it was sitting abandoned and he was paying the taxes out of his retirement check."

"She still wants him to sell the farm," I said. I couldn't believe that Aunt Louise was really trying to help Gramps.

"She thinks it's too much responsibility for him."

"Why? He doesn't have to do anything."

She smiled. "Louise and Edward have a house in Jamestown that they rent out."

I knew that. It was the house Edward lived in before they were married. It was a little house, and when they moved into the big one where they lived now, they had rented the old one instead of selling it.

Mother stood up and walked to the window. "They go to check it over every month, when the rent is due. There's always something that needs to be fixed. A dripping faucet. A leak in the roof. Paint starting to peel. Louise thinks the farm is the same way."

She walked over to the refrigerator and took down a magazine clipping that had been pinned there with a magnet shaped like an apple. "Louise gave me this for Dad. It's about a group called the Nature Conservancy. They buy land to keep it from being developed."

"So she does want him to sell it."

"Actually, she suggested that he donate the farm to them, to be set aside as a park. She said they might name it after your grandmother."

I sat staring into my cereal, ideas whirling in my head. It sounded like a wonderful plan. Like something Gramps might really like to do.

"What does Gramps think about this?" I asked.

Mother took the clipping and stuck it back on the refrigerator. "I don't know. With all that's been happening around here lately I haven't had a chance to talk to him about it. Anyway, you wanted to know what Miss Ryderson will say in her report. People who think others are out to get them are paranoid, so she may say that."

I nodded. "Aunt Louise told her what Gramps said about trying to poison him."

"With too much sugar in the cake? He just meant it wasn't good for us. Not that she was really trying to poison him. But that's just the sort of thing they'd tell a judge."

She gazed out the window for a minute, to where one of the climbing roses had clawed its way up to peek around the window frame like a fat pink face. "Then there's the matter of the fairies," she said.

I waited. I wasn't sure what she was going to say, and I didn't want to make things any worse than they already were.

"Miss Ryderson may feel that your grandfather is losing his grip on reality. It isn't believing in fairies that matters. It's whether he can tell what's real and what's make-believe."

She looked down at her coffee cup, as if she'd suddenly remembered it was there. She tried to smile. "Whatever she's going to say, we'll find out soon. Before she left yesterday she said she didn't think she needed any more tests or observation. I guess we may as well enjoy ourselves until we hear from her."

"Could we go out to the farm for the day?" I asked, thinking of the fairies. "We could take a picnic lunch and take a better look around than we did last time. I think Gramps would like that, and he said the man who rented the pasture didn't mind."

I looked at her expectantly, but she shook her head. "I have a doctor's appointment this morning. It's only a routine checkup, but I won't be able to do anything else until this afternoon. When I get home we'll see what your grandfather wants to do."

Even though it was a beautiful day, nobody was in a very good mood. We sat around the house looking glum until Mother left for her appointment. I guess we all thought the same thing: Miss Ryderson would make her report in a day or so and that would be the end of our good times together.

After Mother left, Jessie brought the coffee can into the front room and let Willow climb out on her hand. The rose was beginning to wilt, so I went outside and cut another one, the pink one that had peered in the kitchen window.

I took the yellow rose out of the can gently, and carried it over to where Gramps was sitting in his old chair, frowning around the unlit pipe he held clamped between his teeth.

"Will you hold this rose while I put the fresh one in the can?" I asked, holding out the wilted yellow blossom. He took it hesitantly, like a new father, all gruff and gentle at the same time. He brushed back a petal to get a better look at the baby fairy.

"What did you kids say you named the little runt?"

"Reed," I said, busy cutting the stem of the pink rose to fit in the can.

Gramps grunted. "Weed is more like it.

Them blue-green wings and that stick of a body . . ."

His voice trailed off. I looked over and saw him gazing down at the tiny creature in his hand. It waved one chubby fist and tried to roll over, but its wings were awkward among the petals.

The pipe drooped in Gramps's mouth and his lips curved into a smile. "Kind of cute, ain't he?"

All of a sudden I couldn't stand it. "I wish we'd never found them," I said, wanting to shout. "I wish they'd stayed in their dumb swamp and left us alone. Why should you have to go away just because of a couple of . . . of dumb dragonflies?"

"Nathan!" Jessie said, her voice sharp with shock. "You take that back!"

Gramps held up the hand that wasn't holding the fairy. "Hush, Jess, it's all right. Nate's upset, same's the rest of us."

He turned to me. "This thing with Miss Ryderson's got nothing to do with Willow and her kid, Nathan. Maybe Louise is right, and it's time to admit I'm getting on toward old. Maybe she ain't. But finding these two . . . Well, they may not be magic like people think fairies ought to be, but they're plumb special, and whatever happens to me now, I'll have them to think on till the day I die. I ain't sorry we found them."

I sat on the arm of his chair, where I could reach to put my arms around his neck. I was trying hard not to cry, but I guess a tear or two got away. "What are we going to do, Gramps? We love you too much to let anyone take you away. We couldn't make it without you."

He put his free arm around me, and when he spoke his voice was gruff. "I felt the same way when I lost your grandmother." His gaze rested a moment on the pipe she had given him so many years ago. "I love you kids, too, more than anything. But we got to take what life brings and make the best of it. You'll do all right, no matter what happens."

He took his arm away and dabbed at his eyes, the way I was dabbing at mine. I forced myself to laugh. "Too bad Willow isn't really magic. We could make a wish that everything would be all right, and it would be."

"Don't you worry none," Gramps said. "Everything will be all right. For now, we got to think about these two. We've got to get them back to the farm before . . ."

I didn't let him finish. Whatever he was going to say, I didn't want to think about it. "I asked Mother if we could go on a picnic to the farm this afternoon. She said she'd ask you when she got home."

Gramps looked over to where Willow was perched on Jessie's shoulder, preening her wings. Then he looked down at Reed, clutching a petal in both tiny hands and sucking at the edge of it. "I'm going to miss the little varmints," he said. He looked at me. "How about if we pack a lunch now so we're all ready to go when she gets home?"

I made tuna fish sandwiches. Jessie set out some apples and cookies while Gramps got the wicker picnic basket down from the hall closet.

"Haven't used this much lately," he commented. "We ought to go on more picnics."

Neither Jessie nor I said anything. We were both afraid this would be our last chance for a picnic together.

I was right in the middle of wrapping the sandwiches when the phone rang. "I'll get it," piped Jessie.

I could hear her clearly in the quiet house. "Mother's not here right now," she told the caller. Then she was quiet for a minute, listening. "I guess that would be all right," she said. "She'll be home about one o'clock."

When she came back into the kitchen I frowned at her. "You know the rules. You can let people talk to Gramps, but you're not supposed to tell them Mother's not here, and never tell them how long she'll be gone."

She nodded her head unhappily. "I know. But that was Miss Ryderson. She wants to talk to Mother. She's going to come over at one o'clock."

Chapter thirteen

At a quarter to one, Miss Ryderson arrived. I pushed the living-room curtains to one side and watched her park on the street in front of the house, leaving the driveway clear for Mother. I had to admit she was more thoughtful than Aunt Louise, who always did what was most convenient for herself.

Then I thought of the article Aunt Louise had given Mother, and I felt confused. I didn't understand Aunt Louise any better than she understood Gramps. That worried me, because Aunt Louise had known Gramps all her life. Miss Ryderson had only had a few days to figure Gramps out, and she was the one who was going to say what would happen to him.

I let the curtain fall back across the window and opened the door.

Miss Ryderson smiled at me. "Hi, Nathan. I'm surprised you're inside on such a beautiful day."

"We were planning a picnic this afternoon." I couldn't help adding, "Before you called."

She stood looking at me, clutching her briefcase in her arms. Finally she stepped past me into the room so I could close the door. "I haven't been on a picnic in years. Not since I was about your age." I thought her voice sounded wistful, the way Mother's did sometimes when she talked about the good times they'd had before my father died.

She set her briefcase on the coffee table. When she turned back toward me, her voice was brisk. "I wish I could go with you. Don't worry, though. I won't be here very long. I just need to see your mother for a minute."

My eyes strayed to the briefcase. Was it full

of forms that had to be signed to send Gramps away? Was that what she had to see Mother about?

"You think I'm a terrible person, don't you?" she asked suddenly.

"No," I said. "I think you have a terrible job."

She sighed. "Sometimes it is terrible. It's not always easy to be sure you're doing the right thing." She looked at me, as serious as could be. "When you're a little older, Nathan, you'll see that things aren't always good or bad, right or wrong. You just have to do what you think is best."

Gramps had said almost the same thing the other night. It was confusing. I liked Miss Ryderson. And I hated her, too, because of what she was going to do.

The door opened and Mother came in. I hadn't even heard her drive up. She had stopped to buy groceries, and she held a big brown paper bag in each arm. Her smile seemed to freeze when she spotted Miss Ryderson.

"Let me help you with that," Miss Ryderson

said, reaching for the groceries. She took one bag and I took the other, leaving Mother to set down her purse and follow us into the kitchen.

"Would you like a cup of coffee?" Mother asked.

"Oh, no thank you," Miss Ryderson said. "I just wanted to stop by and talk to all of you one more time. I'm going to turn in my report Monday, and I thought you'd want to know what it will say."

I held my breath. This was it. We couldn't even wait until Monday. She was going to tell us now and ruin our last picnic.

Gramps leaned forward in his chair. "So what are you going to tell them, missy? Am I a crazy old coot who shouldn't be out on his own?"

Miss Ryderson shook her head. "The only question is whether you might do something to hurt yourself or someone else. I don't find any reason to expect that."

I grabbed Jessie and gave her a big hug. "Gramps can stay!" I was shouting, but nobody noticed. Mother gave Gramps a big hug and kissed him on the forehead, and he wiped his face with his sleeve, like he was embarrassed by the kiss, but I could tell he was wiping tears out of his eyes, too.

"Will you stay and celebrate with us?" Mother asked Miss Ryderson.

"No, I'd better not." She glanced at me. "Nathan said you were going on a picnic this afternoon, so I won't keep you." She looked at the wicker picnic basket on the table. "We had one exactly like that. It belonged to my grandmother when she was first married. It really brings back memories."

Mother patted the basket. "Why don't you come with us?" She looked at me, smiling. "You packed enough for one extra, didn't you, Nathan?"

I wanted to say no, that there was only enough for us, for the four of us, for this special picnic together, but Mother went on without waiting for an answer.

"If not, we can always put in a little more. I bought potato chips and some marshmallows.

Maybe we can build a little fire out by the spring."

"Oh, I couldn't . . ." Miss Ryderson began, but Mother seemed to hear the same longing in her voice that I heard, and Mother wasn't going to ignore it.

Ten minutes later we were all packed into the station wagon, Gramps driving, Mother in the middle and Miss Ryderson sitting next to the window.

Jessie and I sat in the backseat, with Jessie over behind Gramps, as far as she could get from Miss Ryderson, clutching the coffee can full of fairies. Even with Miss Ryderson along, this was going to be our only chance to take them back where they belonged.

Miss Ryderson turned a little in her seat, looking back at Jessie. "What's in the can?" she asked cheerfully.

"Fairies," I answered, grinning at her. I said it the way you might say, "Dinosaurs. What's it to you?" I knew she wouldn't think I really meant it, or I wouldn't have said it.

Mother didn't turn around, but her voice was half pleading, half ordering. "Come on, Nathan, let's knock off the jokes about fairies, okay?"

Miss Ryderson turned back to the window and didn't say anything for a while. I was a little sorry I had hurt her feelings, but I couldn't help wishing she hadn't come along. If she hadn't, we might have been able to tell Mother about Willow and Reed instead of hiding them in the coffee can all the way to the farm.

Gramps drove more slowly than usual. Maybe he was being careful because Miss Ryderson was in the car, or maybe he felt gloomy the way I did about saying good-bye to the fairies. I couldn't tell.

The farm hadn't changed since the last time we were here. It still looked like an old, empty farmhouse on the edge of a green meadow with woods beyond. Somehow, it felt lonely this time. Maybe that was because I didn't expect to come out here again for a long time. Willow and Reed would be nothing but memories, like my father and my grandmother, with no one around but the black-and-white cows.

I shook off the feeling and looked across the meadow toward the spring. Everything was green and gold in the slanting rays of the sun, the spring a splash of silver. I tried to feel happy for the fairies. If it was my home, I'd be glad to be back.

Mother and Miss Ryderson walked up toward the house. Jessie went into the barn. I followed her. "What are we going to do about Willow and Reed?" she asked.

I shrugged. "Leave them here in the barn, I guess, until it's almost time to leave. They'll be safe enough. We don't want to take a chance on anyone seeing them."

I could see tears forming in her eyes. "Look," I said. "Why don't we take them down to the spring now? We can open the can and play around as if we're chasing dragonflies or frogs or something. That will give us a chance to make sure Willow wants to be here."

Gramps came into the barn behind us. "Your mother's showing Miss Ryderson the house. I'll fetch some wood for a fire, and keep them occupied so they don't follow you down to the spring."

He looked at the coffee can. Jessie held it out, taking the cover off first. Gramps gazed down into the can for a long minute. "Good luck, critter," he said softly. "It's been a privilege knowin' you."

He turned and walked off toward the back of the house, where there was an old woodpile. Jessie and I took the path to the spring, feeling the tall grass swish around our legs. We stopped at the same spot we'd stood the last time. We could see ripples in the water where frogs had leaped to hide from us, and the green and brown cattails swayed gently in the breeze.

Jessie took the cover off the coffee can and held her hand out for Willow. The fairy climbed out slowly into the late-afternoon sunshine. Then she looked around and gave a little chirp, and then two more. It was easy to see she was excited. She didn't sit on Jessie's finger the way she usually did. Instead she seemed to dance, her wings humming and her feet barely touching Jessie's hand.

A second later she leaped into the air, still dancing, but now it was a graceful ballet of swoops and glides with her wings flashing in the sunshine. She hovered for a minute in front of Jessie. Then she darted over to me and hovered so close in front of me it made my eyes cross trying to look at her. She reached out one delicate hand and touched my cheek.

"Hey, that tickles," I said, laughing.

Willow moved about a foot away and hovered, chirping.

"I guess she's glad to be home," Jessie said.

"Yeah, she really seems happy," I agreed.

Willow buzzed over to the can and dropped inside. A minute later she reappeared, with Reed tucked under one arm. He looked like an awkward load for her, but he wasn't wiggling much, and she didn't seem to have any trouble carrying him.

She stopped in front of Jessie, hovering the way she had with me. She reached out her other hand and touched Jessie's face. A tear slid down Jessie's cheek, and Willow touched that, too, chirping softly as if to say it was all right.

Jessie gulped and nodded. "Good-bye, Willow. Take good care of Reed."

Willow swooped away, out over the center of the spring, and I heard the buzzing of wings from the reeds along the banks. I couldn't help wondering. There were lots of dragonflies around the spring, but how many fairies? I heard chirping, too, but it was probably crickets. I couldn't tell.

"Come on," I said, picking up the empty coffee can and taking Jessie's hand. "Let's get back up to the house before they come looking for us."

Jessie stood still, staring out over the spring. "She's gone."

"No, Jessie, she's back, back where she belongs."

She nodded. "I know. But we'll never see her

again, will we? I wish we could see her again. I wish we could come and live on the farm."

I did, too. Finding a fairy hadn't exactly made our wishes come true, though.

Jessie followed me up the path toward the house. "Do you think she'll remember her adventure? The trip to our house? And Smokey?"

I laughed. "She'll remember Smokey, all right. I think she'll remember us, too. But she doesn't know where we live, if that's what you mean. She was unconscious on the front of the car going there, and locked up in a coffee can coming back. I hope she won't remember much of that."

"I wish she could have said good-bye to Gramps the way she did with us. He would have liked that."

"Is that your third wish?" I asked, turning to her with a smile.

She smiled back. "I guess so."

"Catch anything?" Mother asked when we got to the house.

I held up the empty coffee can. "No. The frogs heard us coming and the dragonflies were too fast."

They had brought three straight-backed wooden chairs out onto the porch and were watching the sunset. "Why don't you bring the picnic basket and we'll eat here?" Mother suggested.

Miss Ryderson stood up. "I'll help," she said, coming down the worn wooden steps.

"I can do it," I said.

"I know you can," she said, her eyes glinting a little with amusement. She came with me, anyway.

We were almost to the car when she looked off toward the spring. "Are there any fish in there, do you think?"

"Some. My father used to fish there. I remember once he caught a big bass. Almost a record."

"I used to fish with my dad," Miss Ryderson said. "We used grasshoppers for bait."

"Father used hellgrammites."

She nodded. "Dragonfly nymphs. They're good, too."

I stopped with my hand on the back door of the station wagon. "What did you say?"

She looked at me. "Dragonfly nymphs. A lot of people use them for bait."

"Father and Gramps always called them hellgrammites," I said slowly.

"Hellgrammites are dobsonfly larvae, but most people don't know the difference. They look a lot alike. Like a cross between an alligator and a caterpillar."

Nymphs, I thought. Nymphs and sprites and fairies. In the old folktales, they were almost the same thing. Maybe that was because people really *had* seen fairies. Maybe they wanted to let anyone else who saw a fairy know that, but they were afraid to come out and admit that they believed.

Miss Ryderson and I carried the basket between us. We were halfway back to the farmhouse when she stopped and shifted her grip on the picnic basket. "What made you decide it was all right for Gramps to stay with us?" I asked.

"He belongs here with you and your family, Nathan. You and Jessie are good for him." She smiled. "You keep him young."

"What about the way he gets along with our neighbors?"

Miss Ryderson laughed. "Sometimes I think he's just more honest than the rest of us. He says what he really means instead of what people think is polite."

"How about Aunt Louise?" I asked. "Does she really think he'd be better off living in some sort of home?"

She frowned a little. "People are so different. Think of it this way: If you loved chocolate ice cream, and you thought it was the best thing in the world, what kind of ice cream would you get someone else for a special treat?"

"Chocolate," I said instantly.

"But what if they liked strawberry better? What if they didn't even like chocolate?"

I looked at the path, thinking. "So Aunt

Louise wants Gramps to have the things that would make her happy?"

"I think so. I hope my report will convince her he'd be happier the way he is." She paused, then said softly, "Even if he does believe in fairies."

I stopped suddenly. "Did he tell you that?"

She shook her head. "I didn't ask him. You see, Nathan, I don't think that's anyone's business as long as it doesn't interfere with his life. And I can't see that it does."

I grinned. "I'm glad you came along today."

"So am I," she said, grinning back. "Now we'd better get this food up to the house before it's too dark to eat."

The sun was setting as we reached the porch, and we sat around eating in the warm purple-gold of dusk. None of us felt like building a fire, so we ate the marshmallows cold.

When the last of the sandwiches were gone, and most of the cookies, Gramps stood up. "I think I'll walk down to the spring. Anyone want to come along?"

Jessie jumped up and took his hand. "I do."

Mother was picking up the scraps and trash from our lunch. "Nathan, please take the basket to the car first."

I did as I was told, and then started toward the spring. Gramps and Jessie were almost there. Mother and Miss Ryderson were walking more slowly. As I came up behind them, Mother sighed. "I wish we could live out here, the way we did when I was growing up. It's so peaceful."

I caught her hand and walked beside her. "Why couldn't we, Mother? You could have your bookkeeping business out here."

Miss Ryderson spoke up from the other side. "Why not? Most of your business is by telephone, anyway, isn't it? If you had to see clients in town, I'll bet you could work out a deal with my tax accountant to use his office space if you did some work for him, too."

Mother picked a blade of grass and smoothed it between her fingers. I could tell she was considering the idea. "Maybe," she said thoughtfully. "Maybe it would work. I'll have to think about it."

"I want to catch up with Gramps," I said, hurrying on ahead. I had a lot to think about, too. Gramps was staying after all! And maybe we could all come out to live at the farm.

Gramps and Jessie had taken the path on around the spring, and they were standing on the far bank when I caught up. "Have you seen Willow and Reed?" I asked, out of breath from running..

It was so dark I barely saw Jessie shake her head. "No."

"Not yet," Gramps said. "But listen."

We stood there quietly, listening to the sounds of the evening. Mother and Miss Ryderson had stopped on the other side of the spring, and were talking softly, but we couldn't hear what they were saying. Around us the night was alive with other sounds. A frog croaked, and another, farther off, answered him. Crickets chirped in the meadow. A mosquito buzzed in my ear. I swatted it.

"Do you think that Willow and Reed are the

only fairies left, Gramps?" Jessie asked beside me.

"No, honey, that ain't likely."

"Miss Ryderson says dragonfly larvae are called nymphs," I said. "No one would call such an ugly thing the same name they called fairies unless . . ."

"Less'n they seen something like we did, and were afeard folks would think they were crazy? Could be, Nate. I reckon it could be."

"So we aren't the first people who've seen fairies," I said.

"I reckon not. And not likely to be the last, neither."

The moon was rising, round and bright and almost full. I could see clearer now. "Gramps, do you ever think about coming back to the farm to live?" I asked.

I watched his face, silver in the moonlight, with black lines carving it in tiny wrinkles. "Sometimes I wish . . . ," he began, and then stopped, shaking his head. "Not much chance of that."

He cleared his throat and began again, not

looking at me. "But I'm not going to sell it, either. I think I'm going to give it to you."

"To me? But I'm just a kid," I protested.

"It'd be in trust, for when you're grow'd. Then you could move out here to live if you wanted to."

I squeezed his hand, not knowing what to say. I thought of all the things that had happened the last few days, all the wishes we'd made. I had wished that Gramps could stay with us, that everything would be all right. Miss Ryderson had wished she was coming on the picnic with us. And Mother and Jessie and Gramps and I had all wished that we could come back to the farm to live.

The only wishes that weren't coming true were the ones about things that had already happened, like Miss Ryderson never coming to see us and us never finding the fairies. You couldn't change what was past.

Jessie had wished to see Willow again, I thought, looking up at the moon. A delicate dragonfly shape danced across the bright face of it, and then another one, smaller and less graceful, joined the dance. I held my breath, watching.

"Willow," breathed Jessie.

"Yep," Gramps agreed. "Willow an' her kid."

As we stood there gazing up at them, other shapes joined them, and soon the moon was ringed with a flutter of dancing wings.

"They're celebrating," Jessie said. "The fairies are having a party to welcome Willow home."

"Some of them could be dragonflies," I said. "Maybe all of them. It's hard to tell from here."

"Maybe," Gramps said. I could tell he didn't believe it, any more than I did. In the pale glow of the moonlight I thought I saw something hover near his shoulder and brush against his cheek.

"Maybe," he said again.

Maybe they were dragonflies, I thought. But maybe they were fairies, like Willow and Reed. And maybe there really was such a thing as magic.

Edison Twp. Free Pub. Library
North Edison Branch
777 Grove Ave.
Edison, N.J. 08820